The MORE the Merrier

Happy Birthday Danisha

written by Sonya Trevaley

illustrated by Jessica Clerk

Mc Graw Hill **Macmillan McGraw-Hill**

New York   Farmington

Danisha was thinking about Saturday.
She wanted it to be special. Saturday
was her birthday.

"There will be a cake with eight candles," she thought. "We can play games. We can play music and dance. And Dad can do a magic show!"

"Mom?" Danisha asked. "What kind of parties do you like?"

"Big ones," Mrs. Croy said. "The more the merrier!"

"Me too," Danisha said. "I like everything big."

Danisha made a party list. She
started with Anna. Anna was her best
friend. She added more names. With
each new name, she repeated "the
more the merrier."

"I hear Danisha's birthday is this Saturday," said Mrs. Nelson.

"That's right. We're having a party," Mrs. Croy said. "Why don't you and Troy come?"

At school, Danisha asked one friend
after another. By the end of the day,
she had lost count.

She told Anna about her big list.
Anna asked, "Where will people sit?"

Mr. Croy said that he had asked ten people to the party. Mrs. Croy had asked all their neighbors.

"How many do you think is too many?" Mr. Croy asked.

"I'm not sure," Mrs. Croy said.

Then Danisha told them about her party list.

"Is more still merrier?" Danisha asked.

"Yes, it is," Mrs. Croy said, smiling. "But how will we make enough room?"

Mr. Croy glanced around the living room. "I know," he said. "We will empty the room."

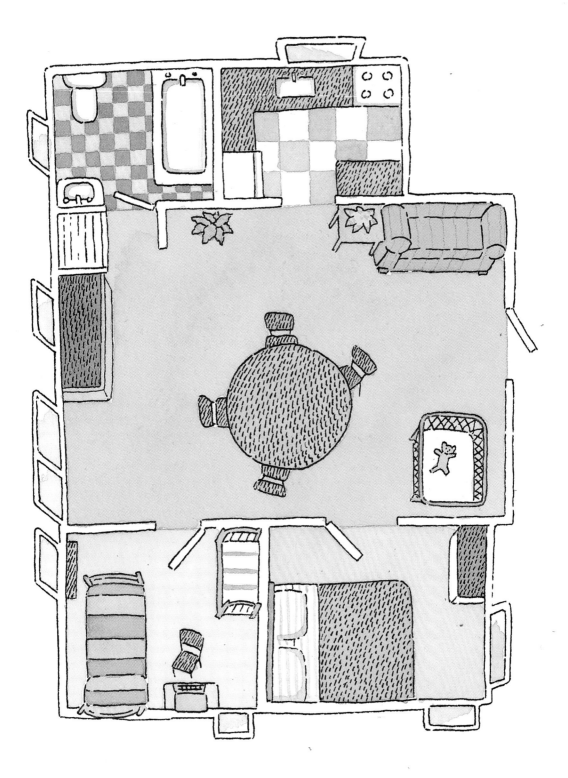

Saturday morning came. The Croy
family got ready for the big party.

Finally, the room was empty. It still
didn't seem big enough.

"We'll have people in every corner of
the house," Mr. Croy said.

"And in the hall, too!" Danisha smiled.

"I don't think the neighbors will get mad," Mrs. Croy said.

"No, they will all be at the party!" cried Danisha.

It was a good party. No one got too
wild. They danced in the living room.
They played games in the hall. Then
they sang "Happy Birthday to You."
They ate cake. Danisha got lots of toys.

Last was the big show.

Mr. Croy put his hat down.

He said, "One, two, three, four. To be merry in the Croy house, we need just one more."

Mr. Croy picked up his hat. Out
popped a little black kitten.
"The more the merrier!" he said.